Little
Brother
and Little Sister

# Little Brother and Little Sister

Retold and Illustrated by

## Barbara Cooney

BARNES
&NOBLE
BOOKS
NEW YORK

This edition published by Barnes & Noble, Inc.,
by arrangement with Bantam Doubleday Dell,
a division of Random House

1999 Barnes & Noble Books

ISBN 0-7607-0694-8

Printed in Spain by Gráficas Estella, S.A.

99 00 01 02 03 04 MC 9 8 7 6 5 4 3 2 1

for Suzie

Once upon a time in a house at the edge of a village, there lived two children, a brother and a sister. They lived with their stepmother, who scolded them from morning until night. To her own daughter, who was as mean as a weasel and ugly and one-eyed as well, she was as sweet as honey. The mother and daughter fed sumptuously on chicken and dumplings and drank frothy golden beer, while the little brother and little sister had only stale bread crusts to eat and water to wash them down. Even the dog ate better than they did.

One day after the noon meal the stepmother and her daughter, full of choice titbits and sleepy from beer, lay down to nap. Outside bees buzzed in the golden sunlight. Soon snores came from the bedroom and from beneath the table where the dog lay. Little Brother took Little Sister's hand.

"Let's run away," he said. "Even the dog is happier here than we are."

They filled their pockets with bread crusts and, hand in hand, set forth into the wide world. Behind them they left the scolding and the pinches, the slaps and the kicks. Ahead lay the forest and the path to freedom.

All the rest of the day they walked. When they reached
the forest the path grew narrower and fainter until finally it
gave out altogether. It grew dark. Rain began to fall and tears
ran down their cheeks. Their brave hearts grew frightened.

They were very tired when at last they came across an old hollow tree. Crawling inside, they nestled together and were asleep immediately.

When they awoke, the sun was already high in the sky
and was shining into the hollow tree. Crawling out, they
yawned, stretched, and sat on a log to eat their bread.

"Oh," sighed Little Brother, "I am so thirsty. If only there were a brook nearby!" He cocked his head and listened hard. "I think I hear water running," he said.

Brushing the crumbs off her skirt, Little Sister followed Little Brother until they came to a sparkling, rippling little brook.

"Listen!" said Little Sister. "The brook is talking."

The brook was murmuring a message:

> "Drink not of me! Drink not of me!
> Or to a tiger changed you'll be."

The water had been enchanted by the wicked stepmother! She was a witch, you see, and in her anger at finding the children gone, she had cast a spell over all the water in the forest.

"I must drink," said Little Brother, kneeling down.

"No! No!" cried Little Sister. "If you do, you will become a ferocious tiger and tear me to pieces."

"Well," said Little Brother reluctantly, for he was very thirsty, "I will wait until we come to another brook."

Soon they came to another brook. As Little Brother knelt to drink, Little Sister heard the brook distinctly say:

"Drink not of me! Drink not of me!
Or to a wolf changed you'll be."

"Oh, please don't drink," said Little Sister. "If you do, you will become a wolf and eat me up."

Once again Little Brother did as his sister wished. And so they went on. Finally they came to a third brook. This time the brook said:

"Drink not of me! Drink not of me!
Or to a fawn changed you'll be."

"Oh, please, Little Brother!" cried Little Sister. "If you drink, you will become a fawn and run away and leave me."

But this time little Brother would not listen. No sooner had one drop passed his lips than he became a fawn.

Little Sister wept, and the fawn beside her wept too.

"Don't cry little fawn," said Little Sister. "I shall never leave you."

She untied her golden garter and fastened it around the little deer's neck. Then she gathered reeds and braided them into a soft leash. This she tied to the garter and, so, leading the fawn, she went deeper into the forest.

After a long time they came to a deserted little house.
"Let's stay here awhile," said Little Sister.
She gathered leaves and moss for a soft bed for the fawn.
Every morning she collected roots and berries and nuts for

herself and tender grass for the little deer, who ate out of her
hand and frolicked about. At night the fawn slept on his bed
of moss, and Little Sister pillowed her head on his back. And
so they lived alone together for a long time in the forest.

Now it happened that the King of the country held a great hunt. The sound of horns, the barking of dogs, and the merry shouting of hunters filled the forest. Hearing them, the fawn was beside himself to join the hunt.

"Oh, please," he said to Little Sister, "let me go!"

He begged so long and so winningly that at last Little Sister gave in.

"But," she said, "be home before dark. I shall lock the door. Knock and say, 'Little Sister, let me in.' Then I will know who it is. If you don't say that, I won't open the door."

At these words, the fawn merrily dashed off into the forest.

When the King and his huntsmen saw the beautiful deer, they gave chase. But the little deer was too fleet for them. When they were sure they had him, he bounded into a thicket and disappeared. At nightfall he ran to the little house, knocked on the door and said, "Little Sister, let me in." The little door opened. In he leaped and slept soundly all night on his moss bed.

But the next morning when the hunt began again and the fawn heard the horns and the "Ho ho" of the hunters, he could no longer rest.

"Sister, let me out," he said.

Once more Little Sister protested, but once more she opened the door. Once more she said, "You must be here by dark. And don't forget the password."

When the King and his huntsmen saw the deer with the golden collar, they again gave chase. Again the fawn was quick and nimble. By nightfall, however, the hunters had surrounded him, and one hunter had managed to wound him slightly in the hoof. This hunter followed as he limped back to the little house and heard the deer say, "Little Sister, let me in." He saw the door open and the deer enter. All this he reported to the King.

Little Sister was frightened when she saw her fawn wounded. She washed off the blood and bandaged his foot with herbs.

"Lie still, little fawn," she said. "And get well."

The wound was so small, however, that when morning came the fawn no longer felt it. When the sounds of the hunt came through the window, the little deer leaped to his feet.

"I must go! I must!" he cried.

"No! No!" begged Little Sister. "This time they will surely kill you, and I will be left all alone in the forest."

"If I don't go, I shall die of misery," pleaded the fawn.

Little Sister, with a heavy heart, opened the door and watched the fawn bound merrily off into the forest.

When the King saw the deer with the golden collar, he said to his men, "You may hunt him all day, but let no one hurt him."

At sunset the King asked to be taken to the little house. There he knocked and said, "Little Sister, let me in." Whereupon Little Sister opened the door. The King entered. The most beautiful maiden he had ever seen stood before him. Little Sister was frightened.

But the King stretched out his hand and said gently,
"Will you come with me to my palace and be my dear wife?"
Little Sister smiled.

"Yes," she said, "but my fawn must come with me. I will
never leave him."

"He shall stay with you as long as you live," said the King.

At that moment the fawn came springing in. Little Sister tied the leash of rushes to the golden collar and led the deer out of the little house.

The King took Little Sister upon his horse. They rode to the palace where they had a splendid wedding. The King and the new Queen lived happily together for a long time, and the fawn romped in the palace garden.

All this time the wicked stepmother had thought that Little Sister surely must have been torn to pieces by wild animals and that Little Brother had been shot by hunters. When she heard about their happiness she was filled with jealousy.

"A queen!" sniffed her daughter. "It is I who should be a queen!"

"Don't worry," said her mother. "I shall fix everything."

One day, when the King was out hunting, the Queen gave birth to a pretty little boy. The witch turned herself into a chambermaid and went into the Queen's bedroom.

"Come," she said, "your bath is ready. It will do you good and help you get strong. Hurry, before it gets too cold."

So the witch and her daughter carried the weak Queen into the bathroom. They put her in the tub, stoked up the fire, shut the door and ran off. The heat was so terrible that the young Queen was soon smothered to death.

Then the witch put a nightcap on her daughter's head, made her get into the Queen's bed, and pulled the covers up so that only her one eye showed.

When the King returned that night he was overjoyed to find he had a son. He hurried to see his wife, but the old witch called out, "Don't open the curtains! The light is still too strong for the Queen. She must rest." So after a quick glance, the King went away and did not discover that a false queen was lying in his wife's bed.

At midnight, when everyone was sleeping, the nurse, sitting by the cradle in the nursery, saw the door open and the true Queen walk in. The Queen took the baby from the cradle and put him to her breast to drink. Then she plumped up his pillow, put the baby down again and covered him with the little quilt. Nor did she forget the fawn. She went to the corner where he lay and stroked his back. Then without a word she went out the door.

The Queen continued to come in the night. Though the nurse saw her, she was afraid to mention it to anyone.

After a time, the Queen began to speak when she came, saying:

> "How is my child? How is my deer?
> Twice more shall I come, then disappear."

The nurse did not answer, but when the Queen had vanished, she went to the King and told him everything.

"Dear God!" said the King. "What can this mean? I will stay with the child myself tonight and watch."

That evening the King went to the nursery. At midnight the Queen appeared and said,

> "How is my child? How is my deer?
> I shall come once more, then disappear."

As before she nursed the child, patted the fawn, and vanished.

The next night the King watched again. Once more at midnight the Queen appeared.

"How is my child? How is my deer?"
I come tonight, then disappear."

The King could no longer restrain himself. He sprang to his feet and took the Queen in his arms.

"You can be no one but my dear wife," he said.

"Yes, I am your dear wife," replied the Queen.

And at that moment she came to life as fresh and rosy and sound as before.

The King had the wicked witch and her daughter tried and sentenced. The daughter was taken to a forest full of wild animals, and the witch was thrown into the fire. When she had burned to ashes, the spell over the fawn was broken, and he became human once again.

And Little Brother and Little Sister lived happily together for the rest of their lives.